My Pet

RABBIT

Kate Petty

Stargazer Books

Rabbits in the wild

Wild rabbits are still a common sight in the countryside. Large groups of them live together in a maze of tunnels called a warren. They come outside to feed on grass and leafy plants.

   These pretty, furry animals make loveable pets. They can live for seven years or more.

Wild rabbits nibbling grass

A wild rabbit in its burrow ▶

Giants and dwarfs

Wild rabbits all have the same gray-brown and white fur, but there are hundreds of different breeds of pet rabbits. There are many colors to choose from and even different kinds of fur.

Some rabbits are giants that weigh as much as 20 pounds (9 kg). Others, like the Netherland Dwarf, weigh just over four pounds (2 kg). Lop-eared rabbits, with their unusual floppy ears, are popular.

New Zealand White

Netherland Dwarf

Even brothers and sisters can be many different colors. ▶

Looking at rabbits

Rabbits have little fluffy tails, called scuts, and long ears. Their ears can swivel in all directions to listen. Sadly, the lop-eared rabbit can't hear as well as other rabbits.

Although a rabbit can see in all directions, it cannot see very far. To compensate, it has a keen sense of smell and constantly twitches its nose as it picks up different scents.

The English rabbit has distinctive butterfly markings.

This rabbit is on the alert. ▶

Bunnyhops

Rabbits can't walk and run like other animals because their back legs are so much longer than their front legs. The back legs are extremely powerful.

Most of the time a rabbit hops about quite slowly, but in an emergency it can sprint away from danger at an extraordinary speed.

The rabbit's hind legs hit the ground in front of its forelegs when it is hopping fast.

A wild rabbit sprinting away from danger ▶

Eating

Grass or hay and a mixture of grains are a rabbit's main food. Vegetable peelings also make a healthy meal. A rabbit's front teeth never stop growing, so it needs a carrot or twig to gnaw on.

Rabbits must always have fresh water to drink. Don't be surprised if you see a rabbit eating its droppings. This helps it to digest its food.

A hay rack keeps the hay clean for this Netherland Dwarf.

An albino French lop eating healthy greens ▶

Friends and enemies

Wild rabbits live in large groups. Pet rabbits need company too. Male rabbits, or bucks, fight each other. But sisters will happily share a hutch and a guinea pig can share with either sex.

Rabbits communicate with each other by thumping on the ground with their back feet. Pet rabbits sometimes do this when they hear you coming.

When this rabbit runs, its bobbing pale scut warns other rabbits of danger.

A Netherland Dwarf on the lookout ▶

Diggers

In the wild, female rabbits, or does, are the chief warren diggers. They have strong paws and sharp claws. They dig with their front paws and kick the earth out behind them with their back paws.

Pet rabbits, both male and female, need wire mesh under the run so they can't burrow their way out.

The Rex, with its velvety fur, is secure in its run.

A wild rabbit digging ▶

Newborn kittens

A mother rabbit builds a nest and lines it with some of her own fur. She usually has six babies. They are called kittens. Newborn kittens are deaf, blind, hairless, and completely helpless.

Kittens will stay in the nest for three weeks, feeding from their mother. By the time they emerge from the nest, their eyes are open and their fur has grown.

This picture shows the size of a day-old kitten against an adult's hand.

Four-day-old Himalayan kittens ▶

Growing up

When young rabbits come out of the nest, they start to feed themselves. They will continue drinking milk from their mother until they are about six to eight weeks old.

After eight weeks, the young rabbits are grown-up enough to go to new homes, but these beautiful babies will still need lots of care and attention from their owners.

A New Zealand White mother with her mixed litter

Week-old kittens beginning to explore their nest ▶

Handle with care

Rabbits are naturally timid creatures and they are easily frightened. Talk gently to a rabbit while it gets used to being handled.

As you pick a rabbit up, rest one hand on its bottom, ready to take the weight. Place your other hand on its neck to steady it. When you put it down, lower its back legs first, as it tends to kick out with them.

The Dutch rabbit is a good size to hold.

An Angora needs careful grooming. ▶

Know your rabbits

There is an enormous variety of breeds among pet rabbits. A rabbit show is the best place to see them all.

Some of the larger breeds might be too big for a child to hold. English rabbits make particularly friendly pets.

Angora

Dutch

Rex

Netherland Dwarf

Dwarf lop

Argente

Black
and Tan

French
lop

Himalayan
Rex

English
lop

Netherland
Dwarf

23

Index

©Aladdin Books Ltd 2006

Produced by **Aladdin Books Ltd**

First published in the
United States in 2006 by
Stargazer Books
c/o The Creative Company
123 South Broad Street
P.O. Box 227
Mankato, Minnesota 56002

Designer: Pete Bennett – PBD
Editor: Rebecca Pash
Illustrator: George Thompson
Picture Research: Cee Weston-Baker

Printed in Malaysia

Photographic credits:
All photographs supplied by Bruce Coleman
Ltd, except cover: PBD

*Library of Congress Cataloging-in-
Publication Data*

Petty, Kate.
    Rabbit / by Kate Petty.
      p. cm. -- (My pet)
    ISBN 1-59604-027-0
      1. Rabbits--Juvenile literature.
      I. Title.

SF453.2.P48 2005
636.932'2--dc22
                                2004063329